ingenious!

injustice!

Geri Halliwell shot to fame with the Spice Girls, a global music phenomenon selling over 55 million CDs.

She has travelled extensively as a United Nations Goodwill Ambassador with particular interest in issues affecting women and children, and she has had two bestselling autobiographies published.

Geri lives in London and has a daughter, Bluebell Madonna.

Books by Geri Halliwell

Ugenia Lavender

Ugenia Lavender and the Terrible Tiger

Ugenia Lavender and the Burning Pants

Ugenia Lavender: Home Alone

Ugenia Lavender and the Temple of Gloom

Ugenia Lavender: The One and Only

uGenia Lavender and the Burning Pants

Geri Halliwell

Illustrated by Rian Hughes

MACMILLAN CHILDREN'S BOOKS

This is a work of fiction. These stories, characters, places and events are all completely made-up, imaginary and absolutely not true.

Ugenia Lavender X

First published 2008 by Macmillan Children's Books

This edition published 2009 by Macmillan Children's Books
a division of Macmillan Publishers Limited
20 New Wharf Road, London N1 9RR
Basingstoke and Oxford
Associated companies throughout the world
www.panmacmillan.com

ISBN 978-0-330-45430-8

Illustrations by Rian Hughes
Brain Squeezers by Amanda Li

1 3 5 7 9 8 6 4 2

A CIP catalogue record for this book is available from the British Library.

Printed and bound in the UK by CPI Mackays, Chatham ME5 8TD

Contents

To Bluebell. Little girl, big imagination.

1

and the Burning Pants

It was Saturday morning. The sun was sparkling like fizzy lemonade.

Ugenia got a phone call from Bronte, one of her best friends.

'Ugenia, I have to go shopping with my mother,' said Bronte. 'Please can you come with me?'

'Sure!' replied Ugenia.

Shopping with Bronte's mum? That sounds important, Ugenia thought.

Ugenia knew that Bronte's parents were divorced when Bronte was a baby, and that Bronte lived alone with her mother. Although Bronte and Ugenia had been friends for a while now, they only ever hung out at Ugenia's house. Bronte had never invited Ugenia round to her house, so Ugenia had no idea what Bronte's mum was like. She thought it was a bit odd, but that maybe Bronte's mum was just a bit shy, like Bronte.

'Granny Betty, I'm going shopping with Bronte,' called Ugenia. Granny Betty had been left in charge while Ugenia's parents were out at the DIY shop.

Ugenia's mum was a presenter on Breakfast TV. Professor Lavender, Ugenia's father, worked at the Dinosaur Museum in town, and he loved anything old and dusty. At the weekends – if Professor Lavender wasn't working – they both loved doing up their house, 13 Cromer Road.

Granny Betty was actually Ugenia's great-grandmother, but she was not your average great-grandmother. In fact, she was more than great – she was extraordinary!

Things you need to know about Granny Betty:

1. She was 101 years old.
2. She treated every day like Christmas.

3. She gave karate chops to anyone who annoyed her.
4. She did wheelies on Ugenia's mountain bike.

'Be a love and pick me up some big white pants at the shops,' grinned Granny Betty, handing Ugenia a five-pound note. 'I really need some new undies – I turned my other big white pants pink in the wash. Oh, and you can keep the change, Ugenia. My little treat.'

'Thanks, Gran, maybe I'll get us some jelly beans as well,' smiled Ugenia gratefully.

Fifty-five minutes later, a shiny red convertible sports car with its roof down and an engine that sounded like it was clearing its throat, skidded into the small drive of 13 Cromer Road, knocking over a flowerpot.

'HURRY UP, UGENIA! HURRY!' shouted a very thin woman from the driving seat. She had a peroxide-blonde beehive hairdo and bright red lipstick.

'This is my mother,' said Bronte, cringing with embarrassment and trying to hide in the back seat.

'Darling, don't call me that! It makes me sound old! Ugenia, do call me Pamela,' said Bronte's mum as she looked into the car mirror and applied even more bright red lipstick.

'Hello, Pamela,' said Ugenia, climbing over the black leather seat and into the back of the car to join Bronte.

'You do realize that today is the most important day of the year?' said Pamela. 'It's the Garrods' summer sale and there will be bargains galore! You'll soon discover, Ugenia, that I love to spend, spend, spend!'

Garrods was a very large department store that sold everything.

'I'm so excited!' shrieked Pamela, speeding off down Boxmore Hill towards the town centre.

Three and a half minutes later, Pamela, Ugenia and Bronte whizzed past the twenty-four-hour, bargain-budget, bulk-buyers' supersized supermarket and finally screeched to a halt outside the large, purple-coloured department store.

'Be a good boy and park it,' purred Pamela as she threw the car keys at a doorman wearing a matching purple coat and top hat.

Pamela – and her now windswept beehive hairdo – marched through Garrods' gigantic glass doors as fast as her six-and-a-half-inch spiky stiletto heels would allow, with Ugenia and Bronte tagging along behind her.

'I want to see the owner – Alfred,' Pamela announced to an assistant. 'Tell him his perfect Pammy is here!'

Before the assistant could move, a tiny, smiling moon-faced man in a purple tailored suit suddenly appeared at the top of a golden escalator.

'Welcome to my universe! How glorious to see my favourite shopaholic once again!' beamed Alfred, descending majestically and giving Pamela an air kiss on both cheeks.

'Alfred, meet my daugh– I mean, my SISTERS – Bronte and Ugenia,' said Pamela.

'Nothing wrong with a little white lie to make you look good,' whispered Pamela to Ugenia.

'Ladies,' declared Alfred, 'let's shop till we drop. Follow me!'

And with that, Bronte, Ugenia and Pamela followed Alfred up the golden escalator.

Ugenia gazed around the store with amazement. This wasn't just any old shop . . . Garrods was spectacular. It sold everything from shoes to sofas, celery to satchels, books to baggage, pants to potatoes. It even sold scented purple toilet paper to wipe pet pooches' bottoms.

There were crowds of people pushing and shoving each other, all trying to reach for the same shiny handbags. It felt like a mad jumble sale, with a mishmash of arms and legs.

This looks like a nightmare, thought Ugenia, staring at Granny Betty's five-pound note. I won't get much change out of this. Everything looks very expensive.

'I want shoes – lots of shoes!' announced Pamela as they entered the shoe department.

'I want every style in every colour!' she purred. 'A girl can never have too many shoes!'

Alfred snapped his fingers. 'Consider it done,' he declared as a mountain of shoeboxes were brought to Pamela's feet.

'I feel fabulous!' shrieked Pamela, parading around the crowded shoe department.

'Now, I want undies – lots of undies!' she announced as they entered the very frilly ladies' underwear department.

'I want every style in every colour,' she purred. 'A girl can never have too many undies!'

Alfred snapped his fingers. 'Your wish is my command!' he laughed, presenting her with an array of multicoloured undies.

'I feel sensational!' gushed Pamela, beaming at herself in the mirror and

hugging the rack of frilly, lacy undies.

Ugenia stared at Pamela's teeny-weeny, dainty panties on their pretty little hangers.

And then she remembered Granny Betty's request.

'Excuse me, Alfred, but do you have any big white pants?' enquired a rather embarrassed Ugenia. 'They're not for me,' she added quickly.

'Alfred, I need you!' interrupted Pamela, who had marched on to the nighties and was stroking racks of pink silk and satin and lace.

'Bronte, I can see why you wanted my support on your mother's shopping trip,'

muttered Ugenia, frowning. 'We might as well not be here!'

Bronte rolled her eyes. 'I think my mum's gone mad,' she whispered to Ugenia. 'She's always slightly crazy, but she can't afford to pay for this stuff – we're on a budget.'

Ugenia felt quite sorry for Bronte. She stared at Granny Betty's five-pound note again.

Suddenly a man with a silver moustache and a giant cigar strolled in. A pair of green-eyed, identical twin girls with white-blonde hair accompanied him.

'Bronte . . . meet Mr Ronald Brump!' shrieked Pamela. 'WE'RE ENGAGED TO BE MARRIED! Surprise!'

Bronte looked at Ugenia. Ugenia looked at Bronte. They both looked at Pamela.

'Isn't he totally, absolutely fabulous?' announced Pamela, beaming at Bronte.

'Don't you just adore him, sweetie? He's a generous billionaire and he just loves to buy me mountains of shoes and handbags, which of course makes me so very happy.' Pamela giggled, clapping her hands joyously.

'We're getting married very soon, so meet your new stepsisters, Vera and Violet!' added Pamela, pointing at the snow-white twins.

'Very nice to meet you,' lied Bronte politely as she went to shake hands with the twins, who were scowling at her coldly.

'I don't think so,' said Vera and Violet in unison.

'I know it's a bit of a shocker as we only met last week, but it's love, Bronte, true love!' said Pamela, throwing her arms around Ronald. 'And he's going to buy me a whopping, huge diamond. He's promised me it's going to be as big as a cherry tomato.'

'Daddy! You said you were going to buy us each a new puppy!' snapped Vera and Violet.

'Yes, of course, my lovely princesses,' gushed Ronald. 'Alfred, can you help my sweet girls, while I escort Pamela to the jewellery department?'

'With the greatest of pleasure! Follow me!' said Alfred, striding into the pet department followed by Vera, Violet, Bronte and Ugenia.

'I want that one,' said Violet, pointing to a fluffy white poodle.

'No, *I* want that one!' said Vera.

'I said it first,' hissed Violet.

'Well I *thought* it first,' snarled Vera.

'He's mine!' shouted Violet, grabbing the poodle.

'Give me that!' screamed Vera, snatching the nervous poodle from Violet.

'Now now, girls, there are plenty of

poodles for everyone,' said Alfred.

'What kind of dog have *you* got?' sneered Vera at Bronte.

Bronte said nothing; her mother would never allow dog hair on the carpet.

'She has a Dalmatian called Dante,' lied Ugenia quickly, desperate to stick up for her friend. 'He has black and white spots, long legs and a very elegant body. He is totally, absolutely fabulous!'

Bronte gave Ugenia a confused look.

'Nothing wrong with a little white lie to

make you look good!' whispered Ugenia to Bronte.

'I WANT A DALMATIAN! GET ME A DALMATIAN!' demanded Vera and Violet in unison, shoving the now terrified poodle into Alfred's arms.

'We don't have any Dalmatians at the moment,' said Alfred hastily, leading the girls away from the puppies and into the garden department.

'How about some lovely roses or lilies?' Alfred asked.

'I'm allergic to roses,' said Violet crossly.

'I'm allergic to lilies,' snapped Vera, glaring at Violet.

'We have an Olympic-sized swimming pool in our back garden!' sneered Vera, turning to Bronte. 'What have you got in

your back garden?'

Bronte said nothing. She only had a garden hose and two broken deckchairs in her back garden.

'Bronte has a sheep in her back garden,' lied Ugenia. 'She's called Shirley. She's all woolly and makes lovely jumpers and she's totally, absolutely fabulous!'

Bronte gave Ugenia a stern look.

'I WANT A SHEEP! GET ME A SHEEP!' demanded Vera and Violet in unison.

'Sorry, no sheep in stock at the moment,' said Alfred, ushering the girls rapidly into the music department.

'Do you like pop or rock music?' he asked.

'I don't like pop,' said Vera crossly.

'I don't like rock,' said Violet, glaring at Vera.

'We play our own music at home,' they said in unison.

'I play the violin,' said Vera.

'I play the viola,' said Violet.

'What kind of instrument do YOU play, Bronte?' sneered Vera.

Bronte said nothing. She had

never played any kind of instrument, as her mother always had a headache.

'Bronte plays the drums,' lied Ugenia. 'She's actually in a band called the Sugar Snaps, and they have a lead singer called Elvis. They are totally, absolutely fabulous!'

Bronte gave Ugenia a horrified look.

'I WANT TO PLAY IN A BAND WITH A SINGER CALLED ELVIS!' yelled Vera and Violet in unison.

'I'm sorry, lovely ladies, your personal shopping time is up and it's back to your devoted parents,' Alfred said, hurrying them along.

He led them back to Ronald Brump who was paying for all of Pamela's new things – including her gigantic, humongous diamond engagement ring, which sparkled like a star

as she waved her hand around proudly.

'Look at the time!' gasped Pamela. 'I must make it to my next appointment. I'm having liposuction on my toes!'

'Bronte and Ugenia – say goodbye to Vera and Violet,' said Pamela, marching off down the golden escalator with twenty bags of shopping. 'You'll see them again next Saturday for the engagement party at our house.'

Bronte looked at Ugenia with horror.

'Goody, we'll get to meet Dante the Dalmatian and Shirley the sheep,' said Violet, sniggering.

'Perhaps we can see you perform in your band, the Sugar Snaps, with the singer called Elvis, if we're really lucky,' sneered Vera.

Bronte said nothing.

'Fine – you'll love everything. It's all totally, absolutely fabulous,' gushed Ugenia to the twins. 'Bronte, meet me at the escalators. I'm just going to give the lovely twins a secret special top tip on how to get along with their new stepmother, Pamela,' said Ugenia.

Bronte wandered away as Ugenia began talking intensely with Vera and Violet.

Two minutes later, Ugenia and Bronte were charging down the golden escalator and climbing into the back of the red convertible sports car. The car was stuffed so high with bags they could hardly move.

Pamela, Bronte and Ugenia sped off back up Boxmore Hill.

'I hope you didn't tell any more lies to the horrid twins? And what do you

mean, *It's all totally, absolutely fabulous*?' Bronte whispered furiously. 'I don't have a Dalmatian called Dante or a sheep named Shirley. I don't play the drums in a band called the Sugar Snaps! And who on earth is ELVIS?' Bronte scowled, trying to keep her voice down.

'I just told a few little white lies to make you look good,' Ugenia whispered back. Bronte hardly ever got cross, but right now she was very, very angry.

'But when Vera and Violet find out it's all lies, they'll be vicious,' groaned Bronte. 'And worse still, my mother is going to marry their dad and they're going to be my horrid stepsisters just like in all those fairy tales!'

'Bronte, you can't believe everything you

read,' said Ugenia, realizing that this was a lot more serious than she had originally imagined. And Vera and Violet WERE absolutely vile.

'What am I going to do?' whimpered Bronte as they approached 13 Cromer Road.

'Leave this to me, I'll fix it,' said Ugenia, who was not really sure how she *was* going to fix it. As the car pulled up at the house, Ugenia gave Bronte a hug, said goodbye to Pamela and leaped out.

'Hello, dear,' said Granny Betty, opening the front door. 'Did you get my big white pants?'

'Big white pants? Oops! Sorry, Gran. I didn't get a chance,' said Ugenia, wondering how on earth she was going to

get Bronte out of the pickle she had landed her in.

'That's OK, dear,' said Granny Betty, 'maybe I can get a pair from my friend Mrs Wisteria. She bulk-buys enormous knickers from the undies stall in the market.'

Then suddenly, like a thunderbolt of lightning, Ugenia had a brainwave.

INSPIRATIONAL! she thought. I'll get some help from *my* friends too! We can make all my white lies true!

'Thanks, Granny Betty!' cried Ugenia, legging it upstairs.

Ugenia immediately rang Rudy and told him everything – all about Dante the Dalmatian, Shirley the sheep, and the Sugar Snaps who had a lead singer called Elvis.

'Who's Elvis?' asked Rudy.

'Oh, he's just some guy I saw singing on my mum's Breakfast TV show last week,' explained Ugenia.

'So what are we going to do?' asked Rudy.

'Rudy, I have a plan. It's a bit of a tricky mission impossible called Borrow to Believe in Bronte!' said Ugenia in her best action-hero, Hunk Roberts voice. 'I need the best people for the job. I need dedication and loyalty. Call Trevor and Bronte right away.'

'I'm on it,' said Rudy.

'Let's all meet tomorrow,' said Ugenia.

Rudy quickly made a couple of calls. Then he pulled out a pack of coloured marker pens and a large vision board and got to work.

☆

First thing next morning, Ugenia showed Trevor and Bronte up to Rudy's bedroom.

'Welcome to our world!' announced Rudy, who was talking on two phones, scribbling on a clipboard and firing off an email on his laptop.

'Troops, take note!' declared Rudy, pointing to his vision board, which read:

BORROW TO BELIEVE IN BRONTE

WHITE LIE 1: BRONTE HAS A DALMATIAN DOG CALLED DANTE.

ACTION: TREVOR TO BORROW DALMATIAN DOG CALLED DAPHNE - SLEEK, BLACK AND WHITE, GORGEOUS PEDIGREE - FROM NEIGHBOUR DAVID DAVENPORT.

WHITE LIE 2: BRONTE HAS A SHEEP IN HER BACK GARDEN CALLED SHIRLEY.

ACTION: UGENIA TO BORROW A SHEEP - FROM BOXMORE HILL PARK.

WHITE LIE 3: BRONTE PLAYS THE DRUMS IN A BAND CALLED THE SUGAR SNAPS, WITH A SINGER CALLED ELVIS.

ACTION: BRONTE TO BORROW DRUM KIT FROM NEIGHBOUR MR MARLEY AND LEARN TO PLAY DRUMS.

EXTRA ACTION: UGENIA TO BORROW ELVIS FROM HER MUM'S TV SHOW.

TOP TIP: BE VERY CHARMING WHEN BORROWING . . . YOU GET MORE FROM HONEY THAN VINEGAR.

EXTRA-SPECIAL TOP TIP: LIE IF NECESSARY.

WE HAVE EXACTLY ONE WEEK TO BE READY!

'Like it?' asked Rudy.

'Love it!' said Ugenia.

'Very nice' said Bronte.

'Er . . . yeah, OK,' said Trevor.

'We have lots to prepare for Saturday!' announced Rudy as he slammed shut his notebook and offered everyone a tarberry juice.

'I'm the designated party-planner,' he added, 'so report to me. Everything must be ready by three o'clock for the party at Bronte's.'

The next Saturday came round very quickly. Ugenia, Rudy, Bronte and Trevor all got up extra early and began to put the Borrow to Believe in Bronte plan into action.

Trevor knocked on David Davenport's door. David owned the Dalmatian dog called Daphne.

But there was no answer.

Hmm, thought Trevor, I'll try my other neighbour, Spike. He's got a white dog, but no one will notice the difference. A dog's a dog, innit?'

Spike was a builder who loved his dog, Savage, very, very much. Savage was a British bulldog. He was extremely chunky, with a squashed-in face that looked like he'd walked into a door.

Spike yanked open his front door and glared down at Trevor. 'Yeah?' he grunted.

'Er . . . I'd love to take Savage out for a long walk today, if that's all right with you?' said Trevor.

Spike's glare immediately changed to a smile. 'Sure,' he replied, 'but mind you take good care of him. He gets really grumpy if his coat gets messy.'

'That's not a Dalmatian!' said Rudy when Trevor turned up with Savage. 'They have black spots and they're tall and slim.'

'No probs,' replied Crazy Trevor, taking

the animal over to Rudy's garage, where he found a big tin of black paint and some brushes among Mr Patel's DIY tools. Crazy Trevor began to paint dainty black spots on Savage's chunky tummy.

Savage growled.

Boxmore Hill Park had big playing fields with swings and, in one area, peacocks, donkeys and sheep.

But when Ugenia got there the gate was shut and she saw a sign.

CLOSED FOR THE WEEKEND
GRASS BEING FERTILIZED
WITH MANURE

Ugenia peered over the gate and saw only mounds of horse poo.

Oh no! No sheep, only poo! Where are all the animals? They must have gone on holiday. Where am I going to get Shirley the sheep from? What am I going to do? thought Ugenia. Maybe I should ask my dad. After all, he is a professor and he is very clever and he knows pretty much everything.

Professor Lavender was working that Saturday, so Ugenia jumped back on her red bike and sped down Boxmore Hill, past the twenty-four-hour, bargain-budget, bulk-buyers' supersized supermarket and into the town centre.

She went straight to the Dinosaur Museum, where her dad worked. It was an old grey building with two stone gargoyles peering down from the roof.

Ugenia wandered through the large, stone building, under the huge diplodocus skeleton, past a stegosaurus horn, down the stairs and along a dusty, dark corridor.

She tiptoed quietly past three men in white coats – including Charlie Darwin, her father's assistant. The men were wearing their do-not-disturb frowns and peering intently down at a tiny piece of what looked like a dinosaur toe.

Ugenia knocked on her father's door, which said:

PROFESSOR
EDWARD LAVENDER
DINOSAUR CONSULTANT
AND
SPECIALIST IN PRETTY
MUCH EVERYTHING ELSE

But there was no reply. Then she saw a note stuck on the door:

OUT OF THE OFFICE – BACK SOON! Prof. L.

Injustice! What am I going to do now? thought Ugenia as she wandered back down the corridor, past the three men who were now staring at an animal with a woolly coat and two big curly horns that was lying on a table.

'Ah, gentlemen, as you can see, we are looking at a very fine specimen of a ram,' said Charlie Darwin. 'Now, our task is to find out whether he could possibly be related in any way to the later dinosaurs.'

'Are rams and dinosaurs related?' enquired Ugenia.

'Well, obviously he's from the sheep family, but this particular breed is very ancient, and we don't yet know when the first specimens walked the earth,' replied Charlie Darwin, looking up at Ugenia.

Suddenly, like a thunderbolt of lightning, Ugenia had a brainwave.

Incredible! This ram is actually just a boy sheep with horns! thought Ugenia.

'Actually, Charlie,' Ugenia said importantly, 'my dad has told me that he

needs the ram for a special experiment. He's asked me to take it home with me right now.' Ugenia decided that this was only a little white lie and it was only to make Bronte look good, right?

'Really?' asked Charlie, looking unsure.

'Oh yes, it's extremely important!' insisted Ugenia. 'That's why he sent me down here.'

'OK, but be gentle. He's quite fragile. He died last week and he's only just been stuffed,' said Charlie.

Before Charlie Darwin could change his mind, Ugenia heaved the huge ram into her arms and dragged it out of the museum. She strapped the ram on to her bike and cycled as fast as she could back up Boxmore Hill to 13 Cromer Road.

Now, I just need to borrow Elvis! she

thought as she hid the ram with her bike at the back of the garage.

Ugenia went into the kitchen. Granny Betty was swinging her hips and gyrating on the kitchen table to some

hip-hop music.

'Granny Betty, where's Mum?'

'Ooh, she's gone to return some wallpaper to the DIY store.'

'Oh no!' groaned Ugenia, 'I need her help to borrow Elvis.'

Granny Betty stopped dancing. 'Ugenia,' she said softly, 'Elvis is dead. He's gone to the great Heartbreak Hotel in the sky.'

'Dead!' exclaimed Ugenia. 'He can't be. I saw him on Mum's breakfast show last week. I need to borrow him for Bronte's band!'

'That wasn't the real Elvis,' said Granny Betty, climbing down from the table. 'It was just someone doing an impersonation of him. And if anyone knows about Elvis, it would be me. Elvis used to be an old friend of mine. We used to write songs and jam together. Have a look in my handbag.'

Ugenia peered into Granny Betty's enormous handbag and found a photo of her gran, looking very young and standing beside a man in a white jumpsuit. His hair was in a big quiff and he had sideburns down each side of his face. He and Granny Betty were smiling at the camera and holding up jars of peanut butter at Boxmore Market.

Suddenly, like a thunderbolt of lightning, Ugenia had a brainwave.

'IMPERSONATION!' cried Ugenia. 'If he was an old friend of yours, Granny Betty, YOU could pretend to be Elvis!'

Granny Betty thought about this for a quarter of a second. 'Sure!' She beamed – she'd do anything for Ugenia. 'I'll just have to apply a little black hair dye, but I think your mum's got some in the bathroom cupboard and it washes out easily. What exactly is this for, Ugenia?'

Granny Betty asked curiously.

'It's for Bronte's mother's engagement party' Ugenia said. 'Her name's Pamela.'

Ugenia took Granny Betty outside and pointed at the large ram strapped to her bike. 'I have this surprise engagement pressie for her.'

'That's lovely, dear,' said Granny Betty, not looking the least surprised as she admired the ram tied on to Ugenia's bike. 'I know Pamela a little. I'm so glad to hear that she's found love again after she split up with her one true love, Derek. He's a local fireman, but he didn't have enough money to buy all the shoes and handbags she wanted, so they fell out. It was such a shame because he really loved her.'

'Wow!' gasped Ugenia. 'That's such a

pity. OK, we'd better get you ready fast, Granny Betty. We're going to be late. It's ten past three!'

Ugenia desperately wanted Vera and Violet to believe in Bronte. But with all the little white lies, anything could go wrong. Thank goodness Ugenia had another special secret plan up her sleeve . . .

☆

To Ugenia's surprise, when she turned up at Bronte's house with her new friend Elvis (Granny Betty disguised in a white jumpsuit and with her hair dyed black), the party was in full swing and going splendidly.

Rudy was handing out trays of cheese and crackers, and crystal glasses, some filled with champagne and some with sparkling tarberry juice.

Bronte was playing the bongo drums with her band the Sugar Snaps. Mr Marley, Bronte's neighbour, was playing bass guitar and Trevor's older sister, Mercedes, was on keyboards. But best of all, Granny Betty started singing with the band, swinging her hips and curling her top lip . . . doing a fantastic impersonation of her friend Elvis.

Everyone seemed to be enjoying themselves.

Ronald Brump with his big cigar and

Pamela with brand-new shoes and a gigantic, sparkling engagement ring were dancing together. Even Violet and Vera seemed to be very impressed and believing in Bronte.

But five minutes later, Vera tapped Bronte on the shoulder. 'Why is Shirley the sheep not moving?' she demanded, staring out into the garden.

'Oh, she's very, very tired. She's been working very hard making jumpers all day,' explained Ugenia.

'I didn't know sheep had horns,' said Violet.

'Duh,' replied Ugenia, 'of course they do. It's a male sheep – didn't you know they could be distant relatives of the dinosaurs?'

'No, I didn't,' said a very puzzled Violet.

At that moment there was a bark at the front door. It was Crazy Trevor with Savage.

'Aah,' said Ugenia, 'that's Dante the Dalmatian. He's just back from the poochie parlour – all specially groomed for the party!'

'He's very fat for a Dalmatian,' said Vera, staring at Savage/Dante, who was salivating at the sight of Pamela and Ronald's enormous, pink seven-layered engagement cake.

'Oh, he has to eat a lot as he's a champion weightlifter. You have heard of the new doggy weightlifting shows, haven't you?' asked Ugenia. 'They're totally, absolutely fabulous.'

'No, I hadn't,' said a very puzzled Vera,

accidentally spilling chocolate mousse all over Savage/Dante's coat.

Savage/Dante growled hysterically at Vera for messing up his coat, and ran furiously into the garden.

'Oooooh noooo!' screamed Violet, running into the garden. 'Dante's attacking Shirley!'

Ugenia, Trevor and Vera followed Violet into the garden to find the ram lying on its

side, stiff as a board. Its stuffing was all over the patio – and hanging from Savage/Dante's mouth!

'Dante's murdered Shirley!' screamed Vera.

'Let's go inside,' said Ugenia quickly, trying to distract Vera and Violet. 'We don't want to upset the party.'

Ugenia ushered them inside to where Bronte was still playing with Elvis/Granny Betty, Mr Marley and Mercedes.

Ronald was just handing Pamela one last gift in a small and beautiful box.

'Diamonds! Is it more diamonds? I love diamonds!' shrieked Pamela excitedly.

'No, sweetness, it's something quite different for you,' said Ronald, smiling and sucking on his cigar. He clearly felt

very pleased with himself.

'The girls – Vera and Violet – told me this is exactly what you wanted.'

Pamela opened the beautiful box and unwrapped the pink tissue paper – to find a large pair of BIG WHITE PANTS!

'Is this what you think I'm worth?' shrieked Pamela angrily.

Vera and Violet giggled with delight.

'Thanks for that special top tip you gave us last week, Ugenia!' whispered Vera. 'What a brilliant way to break up Dad and Pamela!'

'You're welcome,' smiled Ugenia, who had suggested the big pants present back in Garrods, knowing full well how furious Pamela would be.

Still furious, Pamela threw the pants at Ronald's face and they landed on his big cigar.

He brushed them away, tangling them up with his cigar as they flew across the room.

'Bronte!' yelled a very cross Ronald Brump. 'This is all your fault, leading my darling daughters astray with your stupid friends!'

Ugenia and Bronte didn't answer. Suddenly they had noticed a very strong smell of smoke coming from the corner of the room. Ugenia and Bronte peered behind the sofa.

'THE PANTS ARE ON FIRE!' cried Bronte as the big white pants started smouldering and burst into flames. Fire began to climb up the curtains and smoke began to drift across the room.

'OH, DO SHUT UP, YOU STUPID LITTLE GIRL!' roared Ronald Brump, who was too busy to notice any fire as he crawled under the table trying to find his cigar. 'YOU'RE A LIAR! THE PANTS ARE NOT ON FIRE!'

'How DARE you speak to my daughter like that!' snapped Pamela.

'INFERNO!' cried Ugenia, grabbing the hose from the garden and squirting water everywhere. She extinguished the burning pants, soaking Mr Brump and Pamela and everyone else at the party.

72
?

Elvis's black hair dye ran down his face, revealing Granny Betty.

All the black spots on Dante's coat smudged, revealing a charcoal-grey Savage.

Vera and Violet glared at Ugenia and Bronte.

'That is not a real Dalmatian,' said Violet.

'That is not a real Elvis,' said Vera.

'Bronte, you're a liar!' they cried in unison.

Bronte went bright red with embarrassment.

'Bronte's not a liar,' said Ugenia, hanging her head in shame. 'I am. I made it all up because I wanted to help Bronte.'

'Actually, it's me that's the liar,' said Pamela softly.

Ugenia looked at Bronte. Bronte looked at Ugenia. They both looked at Pamela.

'I don't really love you, Ronald,' said Pamela. 'I'm sorry, I lied. It's the jewellery and shoes and handbags that I love.' And she took off the gigantic, sparkling diamond and handed it to him.

'But . . . but . . . but *everyone* loves me!' wailed Ronald.

Suddenly there was a loud siren.

'It's the fire brigade!' exclaimed Bronte. 'I just called them!'

That second, a large fireman in a yellow helmet and a breathing mask strode into the room.

'I see I'm too late! Everything is taken

care of,' said the rather handsome fireman, taking off his helmet and mask and thanking Ugenia, who was still holding the hose.

'Hello, Pamela,' smiled Derek the fireman.

'Hello, Derek, it's so lovely to see you,' gushed Pamela, who was now realizing that she loved Derek more than her jewellery, shoes and handbags.

'Daddy, I want a fire engine! Please can I have a fire engine?' shouted Vera and Violet in unison.

'OH, SHUT UP!' snapped Ronald Brump. 'We're leaving right now. We have to be ready for the Venetian Ball this evening!'

'We're going to the beauty salon!' said Vera.

'We're going dancing!' said Violet.

'What are *you* doing this evening?' sneered Vera at Bronte and Ugenia.

Bronte said nothing. She smiled as she looked at Pamela and Derek.

'Actually, we're going out for a large cheeseburger with our best friend Brian, the zonkoid alien,' said Ugenia. 'HE'S TOTALLY, ABSOLUTELY FABULOUS!'

Big News!

HELLOOOOOO!!! How funny was that! I only just got out of that one OK! It all turned out fine in the end – but only just. I mean, at least Pamela didn't marry someone she didn't love. Now that would be a big fat lie, not a little white one. Thankfully, Bronte doesn't have those weird twins as stepsisters – and yes, they did remind me of the ones in *Cinderella*, but I didn't want to freak Bronte out any further by saying so.

I spent Sunday clearing up the mess at Bronte's house. Pamela's handsome fireman Derek came to help too. Pamela was quite pleased – I could tell as she kept putting on this weird, girlie voice every time she spoke to him. Adults – they can be so funny sometimes!

I'm rambling so I'll shut up!

Big XO

Ugenia Lavender XX

Ingenious Top Tip

The truth always comes out in the wash!

A little water at Pamela's party revealed that Dante was Savage, Shirley was stuffed, Elvis was Granny Betty – and that Pamela didn't love Ronald! But it feels so much better to tell the truth. Lying is hard work!

2

uGenia Lavender

Friday the Thirteenth

It was Friday morning, the thirteenth of July. The sun was already up, burning brightly down on Cromer Road.

Ugenia sprang out of bed as if her pants were on fire. She was ready to wrestle an anaconda snake and take on the world. She was sure it was going to be an especially incredible day.

Why? It was Ugenia's birthday, that's why!

Ugenia stretched in anticipation. She ran to the bathroom, thinking about the presents she would receive – and the cards, the flowers, the cake! If she was *really* lucky maybe she'd even get a puppy! She'd been dropping hints to her parents for weeks.

Ugenia was brushing her teeth and giving herself her extra-special-superstar birthday grin in the bathroom mirror, when she suddenly noticed a strange, large black and white bird tapping at the window.

Hmm, that's an odd-looking bird, thought Ugenia, who felt a bit peculiar as she wandered downstairs in her favourite Hunk Roberts action-hero pyjamas, all ready for her birthday celebrations to begin.

Ugenia's mum had already left for work (she always left before Ugenia was up on weekdays because of her job on Breakfast TV, which started very early). But Ugenia was surprised – and really disappointed – that her dad had left too and was already on his way to the Dinosaur Museum.

So it was Granny Betty who was busily in charge downstairs, frying up a gruesome pile of yesterday's leftover dinner in the kitchen.

'Morning, Ugenia,' Granny Betty said cheerily, 'How are you?'

'Well, it's Friday the thirteenth so it's an extra-special day, right?' smiled Ugenia, waiting for her big happy-birthday congratulations.

'I suppose you could call it special, in a very unlucky sort of way,' exclaimed Granny Betty. 'That's if you choose to believe in that superstitious nonsense, of course. But you're right, Ugenia, Friday the thirteenth is a day like no other, so we'd all better watch our step!'

'What do you mean?' frowned Ugenia, who was beginning to feel a bit frustrated that her birthday hint hadn't worked.

'Well, it's a bit like if you see one single magpie – that would be very unlucky,' said Granny Betty. 'But not if you see two – that would be *lucky*. With magpies it's a case of one for sorrow, two for joy, three for a girl, four for a boy, five for silver, six for gold, seven for a story that's never been told.'

'A magpie? What on earth's a magpie? It all sounds like nonsense.' Ugenia was becoming even more frustrated as this conversation was leading in a very different direction from any birthday congratulations.

'A magpie is a strange, large black and white bird,' said Granny Betty, smiling.

'Injustice!' shrieked Ugenia. 'I've just seen one – it was sitting on the bathroom window ledge! And now you tell me Friday the thirteenth is unlucky too!' Ugenia frowned.

'If you do see a magpie,' Granny Betty went on, 'the way to cancel out the bad luck is to say, "Good morning, Mr Magpie, how's your wife and family?"'

'OK,' said Ugenia doubtfully.

She was hovering over the toaster waiting for her breakfast when she realized that her birthday had been forgotten by everyone in the Lavender family. There wasn't a card or a present or anything. Instead there was just a piece of black toast,

which popped up looking like a chunk of coal and even less appetizing than Granny Betty's gruesome fry-up.

'My toast is burnt!' shrieked Ugenia. 'I knew it, I'm doomed. It's a sign! I might as well go back to bed!'

'Your luck is what you make it. Take this,' said Granny Betty, handing Ugenia a silver charm bracelet which she had been wearing round her tiny wrist. The bracelet had many different delicate things hanging from it, including a silver elephant, a miniature cat, a feather, a little car and a tiny silver daisy. 'It's my lucky charm bracelet,' said Granny Betty. 'It's very precious to me, but you can wear it for good luck. Just don't go walking under any ladders though!' And she laughed.

'Yeah, if you say so! Thanks, Gran,' said Ugenia, who didn't really believe any of this good luck stuff would work, but was willing to try anything. She grabbed the burnt toast and the lucky charm bracelet and dashed upstairs to get ready for school. Another sign of bad luck was having to go to school on her birthday!

Ugenia quickly got dressed and put on Granny Betty's bracelet. Maybe things will get better now I've got my lucky charms on, thought Ugenia.

Ugenia sped to school across Boxmore Hill Green on her red bike. She tried to avoid the dog poo – it would be very bad luck to ride through it (although in France it's good luck to step in dog poo with your left foot, which is weird.

How can you be lucky if you have a stinky left shoe?).

Ugenia tried to feel more positive. Maybe her classmates would remember her birthday? Besides, with her silver lucky charm bracelet on, surely there'd be no more bad luck, right?

Ugenia entered the classroom anticipating big birthday congratulations, but all she got was her usual morning greeting from her best friends.

'What a very nice morning,' said Bronte.

'Oh yes, fabulous weather,' said Rudy.

'Yeah, it's all right, innit,' said Trevor.

There was no mention of Ugenia's birthday as they all prepared for the first lesson of the day – a game of rounders on the school playing field.

Ugenia got changed into her sports kit in the changing rooms, and took off her lucky charm bracelet. For safety she hid it in her left boot, which she left in the changing room, as she joined the rest of the team out on the playing field.

Even though her best mates had forgotten her birthday and it was Friday the thirteenth, Ugenia decided to keep positive and just enjoy the game of rounders they were about to play.

As she got in position to take her turn to bat, Ugenia noticed one single strange, large black and white bird perched in a tree in the orchard next to the field. It was a magpie!

'Injustice!' shrieked Ugenia. 'One magpie again – that's one for sorrow!'

What was it that Granny Betty said I should do to cancel the bad luck? thought Ugenia. Oh yes! 'Good morning,

Mr Magpie, how's your wife and family?' Ugenia called out.

So she was very distracted when the rounders ball came hurtling towards her.

Ugenia took a swift swipe and walloped the ball as hard as she could, sending it flying in the direction of the spectating team players sitting on the bench, who all screamed and ran for cover.

The hard rounders ball zoomed through the air towards Mrs Flitt, their sports teacher. It whacked her straight in the mouth, knocking her two front teeth out.

'Aaaaaaaah!' screamed Mrs Flitt in pain.

'Eeeeeeeeeeeek!' screamed the class in horror as blood dribbled down Mrs Flitt's face.

'Stay right here!' mumbled Mrs Flitt as best she possibly could, dashing towards the gym and leaving the class gasping in panic as they wondered what they were supposed to do next.

'Oh no, it's all my fault!' gasped Ugenia.

'No it wasn't, it was an accident,' said Bronte.

'I hope she's all right – she'll need false teeth,' said Rudy.

'What a shot!' said Crazy Trevor.

If only I hadn't seen that one blasted magpie! If only it wasn't Friday the thirteenth! thought Ugenia, but decided it was best not to share this with anyone as they would think she was a bit crazy.

A moment later, Mr Columbus, the supply teacher, came out.

'Can I have your attention please?' he announced. 'Mrs Flitt has gone to hospital, so calm down and go back inside and get changed and ready for your next class.'

Ugenia and Rudy, Bronte and Crazy Trevor went back to the changing rooms with the rest of the class. Ugenia got dressed quickly and tried not to think about the unhappy Friday the thirteenth birthday she was having.

Oh well, my luck is what I make it, right? Thought Ugenia, trying to be positive. Before she put her boots on, she reached into her left boot for her lucky charm bracelet. But all she found was a sock and some toe fluff.

The lucky charm bracelet was gone.

A horrible feeling hit Ugenia's stomach.

Friday the thirteenth had struck again.

'INJUSTICE!' screamed Ugenia, 'Granny Betty's lucky charm bracelet is missing!'

'Do you think you might have mislaid it?' asked Bronte.

'Do you think it might have been stolen?' asked Rudy.

'Er . . . yeah?' asked Trevor.

'It *must* have been stolen!' cried Ugenia, who began frantically searching through the changing rooms and ripping through people's bags and clothes.

'I want a full investigation!' Ugenia shouted.

'Oi, don't touch that!' said Henry.

'I will find the thief!' cried Ugenia.

'Hey, that's my stuff!' cried Anoushka.

'I'll get to the bottom of this!' shouted a frenzied Ugenia.

'Get off my lunch box!' shouted Max.

The whole class began to get very annoyed with Ugenia, who was now furiously tearing through everyone's pockets.

Suddenly Ugenia saw Lara Slater (who had previously stolen her leading-lady part in the summer play). She was fastening a silver lucky charm bracelet on her wrist. It had many different delicate things hanging from it, including a

silver elephant, a miniature cat, a feather, a little car and a tiny silver daisy!

'Injustice!' screamed Ugenia. 'That's mine! Lara Slater is a thief! She's stolen my bracelet!'

The whole class gasped and stared at Ugenia and Lara Slater.

'Actually, my aunt gave me this for my birthday!' snapped Lara as she shoved the charm bracelet under Ugenia's nose and showed her a silver leaf that had been engraved with tiny-weeny writing: *To Lara, love Auntie Agatha*.

'Satisfied now? I wouldn't go around accusing people without any proof, if I were you,' hissed Lara smugly, and there were murmurs of agreement and disapproving looks from the rest of the class.

Ugenia went bright red as she hung her head in shame. What was happening to her?

This was proving to be the worst day ever. The whole class was annoyed with her, and Granny Betty's lucky charm bracelet was missing. Ugenia's luck was going from bad to worse.

And things did not get any better. Ugenia accidentally spilt pink paint over her teacher, Mr Monet, in art class. She got told off for chatting at the back in maths. She was last in the queue at lunch so all the spaghetti was gone, which meant she was left with Hungarian goulash. And then in her spelling test Ugenia got caught copying the answers she had written on her legs, so was given a detention.

But the worst thing was that not one

person wished her a happy birthday. Everyone – including her best friends, Rudy, Bronte, and Crazy Trevor – had forgotten.

Ugenia asked them what they were doing later, but they all said they were too busy to do anything with her.

By the end of the day Ugenia felt awful. This is happening for one reason only, she thought. Friday the thirteenth is a really unlucky day. Somehow I need to change my luck. Hmm, maybe I should ask my dad. After all, he is a professor and he is very clever and he knows pretty much everything.

When school was over, Ugenia jumped on her red bike and sped down Boxmore Hill, past the twenty-four-hour, bargain-budget, bulk-buyers' supersized supermarket and into the town centre. She went straight to the Dinosaur Museum to find her dad.

Ugenia wandered through the large, stone building, under the huge diplodocus skeleton, past a stegosaurus horn, down the stairs and along a dusty, dark corridor.

She tiptoed quietly past three men in white coats – including Charlie Darwin, her father's assistant. They all wore do-not-disturb frowns as they peered down intently at a tiny piece of what looked like a dinosaur tail.

Ugenia knocked on her father's door, which said:

PROFESSOR
EDWARD LAVENDER
DINOSAUR CONSULTANT
AND
SPECIALIST IN PRETTY
MUCH EVERYTHING ELSE

'Enter!' called Professor Lavender.

'Ah, Ugenia!' he exclaimed, looking pleased to see her. 'Is it about that brontosaurus bogey we were discussing yesterday?'

'No, Dad, it's something else . . .'

Ugenia quickly told her father everything about this unlucky Friday the thirteenth – about the one magpie, the lost lucky charm

bracelet, and about Mrs Flitt's broken teeth. (Well, Ugenia told him *almost* everything. She didn't mention it was her birthday. She couldn't quite bring herself to add more misery to the day by reminding herself that even her dad had forgotten, like everyone else.)

Professor Lavender paused for a moment. His eyebrows knitted together as if they were in a secret conference with each other.

'Aha! It's a voodoo jinx. It's black Friday, that's your problem!' he exclaimed. 'It's a bit like the Hadoo Hanuka Hoola Hoola tribe in the South Pacific. When they go through bad times and believe they are attracting the worst weather, they call upon a medicine man with a lucky talisman to switch their frequency. He performs a series of ancient

rituals to ward off evil. Apparently the weather invariably changes after that.'

'So what does that mean for me?' said Ugenia, who was extremely puzzled.

'It basically means you have to *believe* in the power of good-luck charms and rituals. A lucky charm like Granny Betty's will be much, much stronger if you really believe in it. There are all sorts of things that people do to have good luck,' Professor Lavender went on, pulling down a dusty old green book from the shelf. It was titled *I Should Be so Lucky: the Hadoo Hanuka Hoola Hoola's Supersonic Charms for the Restless*. 'The wisdom of these tribes says that if

you really believe in a good luck charm, then it can be fifty times stronger than if you don't fully believe.'

Ugenia stared at the dusty old green book. 'Ingenious! So what I need to do is believe in the power of things that can bring me good luck. Thanks, Dad. This book looks fascinating. Can I take a look?'

'Yes, sure – I'll be back in a minute and we can take a look at it together. But first I need to check on Charlie. He's analysing some carbonized flesh from a T. rex's collarbone.'

As soon as Professor Lavender left his office, Ugenia decided she had no time to waste in turning her day back into a lucky one, so she stuffed the dusty green book into her yellow rucksack and

headed out the door.

'You know, Ugenia, I was just thinking – all that lucky charm stuff can get a bit silly and complicated,' Professor Lavender called after her. 'It could actually cause more harm than good, so it's probably best not to take it all too seriously.' But Ugenia was already halfway down the corridor – and too far away to hear.

Once outside, Ugenia jumped on her bike and sped back up Boxmore Hill. She sat on a bench on the green and quickly opened the dusty old book.

There was still time to change her birthday luck. And this time she would really try to believe in it – that would obviously make a huge difference. Her dad said that totally believing in a lucky charm would make it fifty times stronger, right? Ugenia stared at the first page of the book. It read:

I should be so lucky!

THINGS THAT BRING ON THE LUCKY STUFF:

~ A black cat crossing your path

~ Touching wood

~ Rubbing stinging nettles on a bald head

THINGS TO AVOID IF YOU DON'T WANT BAD LUCK:

~ Walking on cracks in the pavement

~ Spilling salt

(Throw more salt over your left shoulder to cancel out the bad luck)

~ Putting new shoes on a table
~ Breaking mirrors
(Bury a piece of the broken mirror in mud to cancel out the bad luck)

Ugenia studied the list and began to ponder what she could do to turn this unlucky Friday the thirteenth around.

Suddenly, as she sat there, Ugenia saw lots of magpies fly down on to the green. She counted them rapidly.

'Seven magpies!' she exclaimed. 'What does *that* mean?' And Ugenia went through what Granny Betty had told her: 'One for sorrow, two for joy, three for a girl, four for a boy, five for silver, six for gold, seven for a story that's never been told.'

Ugenia tried to think of what *hadn't* been said. First, there had been no happy birthday greetings. Then she remembered how her day had got worse since the charm bracelet was lost, and how she had mistakenly accused Lara of pinching it.

Suddenly, like a thunderbolt of lightning, Ugenia had a brainwave.

'Incredible! I never said sorry! I should have said it earlier!'

Ugenia was about to jump on her red bike – but then stopped as she stared at the

cracks on the path. She picked up her bike and began hopping along, trying to avoid any cracks. She hopped all the way over the green to the small crescent across the road where Lara Slater lived.

Just then Ugenia saw a black cat coming towards her! Desperately, she ran in front of it so it would cross her path.

'Now all I need is some wood – and a bald head!' pronounced Ugenia. 'Then everything will be all right.' And she quickly touched a tree as she approached Lara's very smart house.

Ugenia parked her bike by the mermaid fountain in the middle of Lara Slater's gravelly front drive. She squirmed a little as she knocked on the front door. It wasn't easy to apologize to Lara, who had always been such a big-headed show-off and looked down her nose at Ugenia.

Lara answered the door.

'Lara, I have to tell you something,' announced Ugenia bravely. 'I was so busy thinking about the unlucky day I was having because it's Friday the thirteenth, and it's my birthday, that I just jumped in and accused you of stealing my silver lucky charm bracelet without any proof, and for that I am sorry.'

Lara stared at Ugenia in shock.

'Really? Gosh, thanks, Ugenia! Well, in that case, I'm sorry too. I shouldn't have snapped. It sounds like you were having a really bad day. Since it's your birthday, would you like to come in and have some tarberry juice?'

Ugenia hesitated – she couldn't believe Lara was being so nice. But then she decided the Hadoo Hanuka Hoola Hoola charms must already be working. And that really, really believing in them was already making them fifty times stronger, just like her father had said. Maybe my luck's already changing, thought Ugenia excitedly.

Ugenia stepped inside, and was just drinking a large glass of tarberry juice and telling Lara how she longed for a new puppy, which she had no chance of getting for her birthday, when Lara's parents, Duncan and Mildred, came in. Duncan was wearing his policeman's uniform and Mildred had bags of shopping with her.

After they'd said hello to Ugenia,

Mildred took out a brand-new pair of shoes she'd just bought and went to place them on the table so Lara could see them.

'No! That's bad luck!' cried Ugenia as she lunged forward and grabbed the shoes from Lara's mother, who then lost her balance and knocked the salt shaker that was on the table on to the floor, showering salt everywhere.

Ugenia knelt down and frantically scooped a handful of salt over her left shoulder. Lara was right behind her, and the salt shot straight into her eyes.

Lara began to howl wildly and crashed into a mirror hanging on the wall. The mirror fell down and immediately shattered on the floor.

Ugenia gasped in horror and quickly

grabbed a piece of mirror and ran into the garden, desperate to bury it in the mud.

'What on earth is going on?' yelled Lara's father as he stormed after Ugenia.

Ugenia's luck was certainly changing. It was getting WORSE!

'I'm so sorry, Mr Slater, I'm just doing a Hadoo Hanuka Hoola Hoola ritual to make things better!' exclaimed Ugenia, still busily continuing to dig a hole in a flower-bed so that she could bury a piece of mirror.

Suddenly Duncan removed his helmet and revealed a very shiny bald head.

Ugenia stared at the stinging nettles at the back of the flower-bed – and then at Duncan's bald head.

'Desperation!' cried Ugenia as she quickly grabbed a large leaf off a plant,

wrapped it round her hand for protection and snatched a clump of stinging nettles.

Lara and Mildred watched out of the window in horror as, quick as a flash, Ugenia leaped up and rubbed the nettles on Duncan's head.

'Aaaaaaaagh!' screamed Duncan. 'What are you doing, you crazy girl!'

'It's meant to bring good luck!' cried Ugenia.

'I'm sorry,' said Duncan, through gritted teeth and with a very sore head, 'but I think it's best for everyone if you take your luck and go!'

Lara and Mildred glared at Ugenia in disbelief.

Ugenia hung her head in shame as she left Lara's house. The *I Should Be so Lucky* Hadoo Hanuka Hoola Hoola charm book obviously didn't work. In fact, it had definitely made things even worse.

Ugenia had taken the book out of her backpack and was just about to throw it in the bin when she realized that her red bike, which she'd left by the fountain in the front garden, was missing.

'Nooo!' cried Ugenia, who couldn't face knocking on the Slaters' front door ever again.

Ugenia stormed back across the green to 13 Cromer Road, without avoiding any of the cracks in the pavement. She had

decided that this lucky charm thing was a load of rubbish and that there was only one thing to do – go back to bed until Friday the thirteenth was over, and before it could bring her any more bad luck.

Ugenia knocked on the front door. Granny Betty opened it, gave Ugenia a quick hug and immediately rushed back to the kitchen. Ugenia followed Granny Betty who seemed very preoccupied with her cooking.

'Gran, where are Mum and Dad? Shouldn't they be back by now?' asked Ugenia.

'Ah, they're a little bit busy today – they'll be home later. Would you like a sandwich?' Granny Betty asked, looking carefully at Ugenia. 'Are you OK, dear?'

'I'm OK, I'm just not hungry,' mumbled Ugenia. But the truth was that she felt awful. Absolutely everything had gone wrong – and she hadn't even told Granny Betty yet that she'd lost the silver lucky charm bracelet that she'd only just been given.

Ugenia felt extremely glum as she trudged upstairs. This definitely had to be the worst birthday in the history of the world. There had been no birthday congratulations, no presents, no cards, no party, no cake, no candles – and definitely no puppy.

Even though it was a warm summer's day and only six o'clock in the evening, Ugenia climbed into bed and pulled the covers over her head. She lay there in

misery, trying to wish away this Friday-the-thirteenth birthday disaster as fast as possible.

Suddenly Ugenia heard a rustling.

She peered over the duvet and held her breath. There on the sill outside her open window were two magpies. Ugenia tried to ignore them as she had decided not to believe in all that good-luck rubbish. But she couldn't help trying to remember what Granny Betty had said. 'What do two magpies mean? *One for sorrow, two for joy*,' whispered Ugenia.

And then one of the magpies hopped

through the
window with
something
shiny
and
silver
in its mouth. It plopped Granny Betty's silver lucky charm bracelet with the many different delicate things hanging from it, including a silver elephant, a miniature cat, a feather, a little car and a tiny silver daisy on to her bookshelf and then flew out through the window again.

Ugenia sat bolt upright in excitement. She leaped out of bed and snatched up the lucky charm bracelet.

Excitedly she ran downstairs and into the living room.

'SURPRISE! HAPPY BIRTHDAY!' shouted all Ugenia's family and friends.

Ugenia gasped in delight as her mum and dad, Uncle Harry, Rudy, Bronte, Crazy Trevor and toothless Mrs Flitt – with almost half Ugenia's class – began singing happy birthday to her, and Granny Betty brought in a beautiful big chocolate cake (which it turned out she'd been making all day).

Ugenia closed her eyes and, as she made her wish, thought how Granny Betty had said that you make your own luck.

'Happy birthday, Ugenia,' said Mum, beaming and giving her a big hug.

'Happy birthday, sweetheart,' said Dad. 'We're so sorry it all went wrong for you today. We wanted to give you a

HAPPY SURPRISE BIRTHDAY!
AZBO
72

big surprise and we've been busy all day trying to get you the perfect puppy, but we haven't had any luck finding just the right one. We've got some other things for you though!' And he stood aside, revealing a mountain of cards and presents in the corner of the room.

Ugenia started ripping the presents open. Among other things there were roller skates, new boots, a cool MP3 player, a brand-new and luminous yellow rucksack to replace her battered old one, chocolate – and her very own silver lucky charm bracelet!

'I am truly very lucky to have great family and friends like you!' Ugenia said, and she smiled with gratitude and went round to give everyone a hug.

Suddenly there was a knock at the front door and in came Lara Slater and her father, Duncan.

'Hi, Ugenia,' said Lara, 'we've come to return your bike. My little brother had borrowed it without asking. Sorry about that.'

'Wow, thanks,' Ugenia said, smiling gratefully.

'And there's one other thing,' Duncan added. 'I realize now that you were upset when you were round at our house earlier, and that's why things went a bit awry. Lara told me what a bad day you were having and, since it's your birthday, I had a word with your mum and dad and they said it was OK . . . so we've organized something that's hopefully going to make this an

extra-special birthday after all . . .'

And there, hiding behind Duncan's leg, was a scruffy little puppy with a rather long and licky tongue.

'I got him a week ago at the dog pound,' Duncan said. 'I rather fell in love with him and he's had a bit of bad luck himself. Sadly, though, we just can't keep him, because we've discovered that Mildred's allergic to dog hair, so we're going to get Lara and her brother a hamster instead.'

Lara grinned at Ugenia.

'I'm going to call him Lucky,' Ugenia said proudly.

'Happy birthday, Ugenia – meet your new dog, Lucky!' said her mum.

'My birthday wish – it came true! Now I *really* feel lucky!' beamed Ugenia as she bounced up and down like a basketball player who's swallowed a pack of batteries. Then she knelt on the floor and gently gave Lucky a big hug.

'Hello, Lucky, welcome to the Lavender family. This has turned out to be the luckiest Friday-the-thirteenth birthday ever!'

Ugenia was just about to take Lucky out into the garden when something outside the window caught her attention. She began counting . . .

'Er, Granny Betty . . . what do *nineteen* magpies mean?' asked Ugenia.

Big News!

Hello, people . . .

Did you guess all along that I was going to get a surprise? I didn't! I had no idea – I just thought everyone was too selfish and too busy to remember my birthday. I was completely wrong!

Just you wait until you meet

my new dog – he's gorgeous. I'm probably going to change his name though. He just loves to misbehave, so maybe I'll call him Misfit!

In the end I had a really great birthday. And for those of you that didn't know or forgot – yes, my birthday is on the thirteenth of July, so put it in your diary for next year. No excuses!

What else . . . OK – pressies. This is what I got for my birthday:

1 puppy – Lucky/Misfit
1 set of roller skates
1 silver lucky charm bracelet

1 MP3 player

1 notebook – for writing my Big
News in!

1 luminous rucksack

1 pair of golden tiger earrings
– hello, girls!

1 pot of my own silver nail varnish
– no more using my mum's

1 new pair of furry boots!!!!
So cool

3 pairs of knickers

1 torch with batteries, so no more
using my dad's!

1 magnifying glass – it's wicked!
Excellent for investigations and
missions impossible!

2 Hunk Roberts movies –

Jamira Vampira – the Black Widow Killer and *The Return of Jamira Vampira.*

Chocolate – lots!

Anyway, I've got to take Misfit out for a pee now . . .

Big X0

Ugenia Lavender xx

Ingenious Top Tip

An attitude of gratitude is very lucky

I think the Hadoo Hanuka Hoola Hoola tribe is right – if you believe in something it makes your luck fifty times stronger. But the really lucky stuff comes when I start feeling grateful for what I have in my life – like all my family and friends. Now that's lucky!

3

Ugenia Lavender

And the Winner Is . . .

It was a warm summer's morning. A tepid breeze trickled through Ugenia's bedroom window, gently whispering that it was time to get up.

Ugenia dozed and smiled cosily as she snuggled under her duvet – until her new puppy, Misfit, jumped on to the bed and reminded her with a huge slobbery lick that it really was time to get up.

Misfit had a rather long tongue that was

too big for his mouth and he had originally been called Lucky, but had already turned out to be a little bit mischievous – especially when he accidentally did a poo in her dad's shoe or outside his office, which made Professor Lavender very cross. Ugenia was convinced the only reason Misfit did things like that was because he sensed that her dad didn't really like him.

Professor Lavender was more into dinosaurs than dogs.

Misfit loved Ugenia and Ugenia loved Misfit – except when he woke her up with his really stinky breath and a big slobbery

lick as if to say, 'I *really* need to go outside for a pee.'

'Aargh, Misfit, get off!' cried Ugenia now as she leaped off the bed and ran to the bathroom. 'I'm sorry, Misfit, you'll have to wait. I'll let you out in the garden in a minute.'

Ugenia was feeling quite perky – everything in her life was running smoothly. She was getting on fine with her friends Rudy, Crazy Trevor and Bronte, and school was going relatively well. In general everything was pretty pleasant – Ugenia had nothing in particular to complain about.

She slipped on her jeans, ate some nicely buttered toast and said goodbye to Granny Betty, who was in charge that morning

since both Ugenia's parents were already at work. Then she slung her new luminous yellow rucksack over her shoulders, jumped on her red bike and headed for Boxmore Hill School.

Everything's just great – there are no problems, no tricky situations, no missions impossible to do. My life is going peacefully and smoothly for a change, thought Ugenia as she entered the school, parked her bike and went into her classroom.

As Ugenia entered the room, Rudy, Bronte, Crazy Trevor and the rest of the class seemed to be buzzing in deep conversation.

Ugenia couldn't help notice that there was a charge of excitement in the air. *Hmm, what's going on? And why don't I*

know about it? thought Ugenia. She was just about to ask someone what was up, when suddenly a screwed-up piece of paper landed on her desk.

Ugenia unfolded it. It said:

BOXMORE HILL SCHOOL'S SUMMER OLYMPICS

- Do you have what it takes?
- Are you a team player?
- Maybe you could take part in the biggest competition of the year!

See Mrs Flitt today if you wish to take part in the first round of tryouts . . .

EVENTS:
100-Metre Sprint
Relay Race
Long Jump
Egg-and-Spoon Race
Obstacle Course

(Please remember: although it is good to be in physical shape, it is also important to be in good mental shape!)

THERE ARE TROPHIES TO BE WON!

Ugenia stared at the words 'There are trophies to be won!'

'Hey, Ugenia, have you seen the flyer for the Olympics?' asked Bronte.

'I'm gonna try out for the obstacle race,' said Rudy.

'The egg and spoon would be very nice,' said Bronte.

'The long jump sounds all right,' said Crazy Trevor.

'What are you gonna do, Ugenia?' asked Rudy.

Ugenia thought again for a split second about the words 'there are trophies to be won' and was just about to jump in with a gush of excitement about wanting to win one, but then hesitated . . . What exactly am I good at? she wondered.

'We could all do the relay race!' said Rudy.

'Very nice,' said Bronte.

'Yeah, all right,' said Crazy Trevor.

'Er, maybe,' said Ugenia.

'What do you mean *maybe*?' cried Rudy. He was puzzled because Ugenia normally loved a challenge.

'Er, I'm not really sure which event is my thing, to be honest,' said Ugenia. 'I'll have a think about it.'

'Well, don't take too long. The trials start tomorrow and if you want to take part then you have to show up!'

So Ugenia went through the day with her mates as usual and tried to ignore the constant chit-chat about the Olympics, the finals of which would take place on the last

Monday of term. Ugenia was just getting used to the feeling of not having any mission-impossible problems to solve or any challenges to work for, and she didn't feel like taking on any new ones right now.

After school Ugenia went round to Granny Betty's house. Not only was Granny Betty 101 years old, she was also amazing at giving good advice. Ugenia went straight round to the back garden, where Granny Betty just so happened to be tightrope walking on the washing line, holding a broom to balance.

'Hello there, Ugenia! How was your day?' beamed Granny Betty.

'OK, I guess. Well, actually, if I really think about it, I feel a bit anxious,' said Ugenia.

'What's wrong?'

Ugenia told Granny Betty all about the Boxmore Hill School Olympics and how she didn't think she would participate, especially since she wasn't really very

good at anything athletic. And besides, she always managed to get herself in a bit of a pickle every time a new challenge came along.

'Quite honestly, Gran, although the thought of winning a trophy is spectacular, what if I don't win anything? It will be just a big waste of time and I'll be one big loser,' Ugenia said softly.

'Follow me' said Granny Betty as she hopped down from the washing line and walked to the green wooden tool-shed at the bottom of the garden.

The tool-shed was used as a carpenter's workshop by Granny Betty's late husband (Ugenia's great-grandad), Freddy Lavender. The shed still contained a few rusty old garden tools among the dusty cobwebs.

Granny Betty weaved her way between the lawn mower, a large rusty saw and a rickety old bike that had flat tyres, towards a glass cabinet that was hiding at the back of the shed. The glass was a bit murky, so you couldn't exactly see what was in there, except that it was something shiny.

Granny Betty reached up to a mouldy jug on the shelf above the cabinet and tipped out a curly silver key. Ugenia held her breath in anticipation as Granny Betty put the key in the lock of the cabinet.

'These belonged to your great-grandfather, Freddy Lavender,' said Granny Betty as she opened the cabinet door and revealed a large photo of Ugenia's great-grandad. He had a beaming smile on his face. The photo was surrounded by dozens

of different gleaming trophies of all shapes and sizes. They were displayed like a beautiful shrine on shelves lined with velvet.

'Wow, that's amazing,' said Ugenia as she stared awestruck at the sparkling silver cups and statues, which were all engraved with Freddy Lavender's name. 'What are they all for?' she asked.

'All sorts, Ugenia. Your great-grandfather was a jack of all trades. Once he put his mind to something, he could turn his hand to anything. Now let me see – there's the Champion Golfer of Boxmore award, the Hole in One

trophy, the Old Timers' Swimming Club championship, boxing, darts, bowling, the Most Original Rose at the Boxmore Flower Show, ballroom dancing, best Victoria sponge-cake, biggest leek, fly fishing and the Champion Pie Eater medal (forty in under a minute) and of course there was his running too,' gushed Granny Betty, who suddenly drifted off a bit as she began daydreaming about her late husband, who she still loved very much.

'It's very impressive. He sounds like he was good at everything,' said Ugenia wistfully.

'On the contrary, Ugenia, he really wasn't brilliant at everything, but he always tried his best, and he had this motto – carpe diem.'

'Carpe diem? What does that mean?'

'It's Latin, which is a very ancient language. It means *seize the day* – in other words, grab your opportunities. A bit like your school is doing with its Olympics.'

Ugenia stared at the trophies and the picture of her great-grandfather, Freddy Lavender, who had a white moustache and twinkling grey eyes.

Then suddenly, like a thunderbolt of lightning, Ugenia had a brainwave. 'Inspirational!' she cried. 'Carpe diem! I'm gonna seize the day! Gran, can I use your phone? I have to call Rudy!'

'Sure,' said Granny Betty, smiling. She was delighted Ugenia had decided to go for it.

Back inside the house, Ugenia grabbed the phone and quickly punched in Rudy's number.

'Hello, Rudy, it's Ugenia. You can count on me. I'm in! I'll be there for the trials tomorrow.'

After lunch the next day, the Boxmore Hill School Olympics practice events began. The mood on the playing field was electric as Mrs Flitt blew her whistle.

Ugenia felt awful whenever she saw Mrs Flitt. Last week Ugenia had accidentally whacked the rounders ball very hard and it had knocked out Mrs Flitt's two front teeth. Although she wasn't angry at Ugenia, Mrs Flitt now had two false teeth, which made her speak with an odd lisp, and every time

Ugenia saw her she remembered what had happened.

Rudy, Bronte, Crazy Trevor and Ugenia got ready to show Mrs Flitt how fast they were and what events they were intending to go in for on the big day. It would take all afternoon to get through all the races, and Mrs Flitt would then decide who would be in the final event and have a chance to win a trophy.

Rudy was a very fast runner and very nimble, and he won his obstacle race with ease. Crazy Trevor did an almighty leap into the sandpit in the long jump, and Bronte held her egg and spoon magnificently, taking them all through into the final races that would take place at the end of term.

Ugenia, however, was not so fortunate. She entered the hundred-metre sprint and came second to last out of twenty people, and she tripped over during the long jump and dropped her egg in the egg-and-spoon race.

There was one final event, which was the relay race. It involved four people in each team. Each person would have to run fifty metres and then pass on the baton to their team mate, until all four people had run.

As Mrs Flitt said, 'On your marks, get set, go!' Bronte ran like the wind and then quickly passed the baton to Crazy Trevor, who ran faster than he'd ever run before.

Crazy Trevor then passed the baton on to Rudy, who ran as fast as a bionic steam train until he was way ahead of everyone else. Rudy swiftly handed the baton to Ugenia, who now had a huge head start over the other teams as Rudy had been so fast.

Ugenia grabbed the baton and began to run as fast as she could . . . but suddenly she could feel the other runners catching up behind her. She could almost feel Henry, Sebastian, Liberty and Chantelle's breath on her shoulders as they began to overtake her. Ugenia desperately tried to lunge forward as she crossed the finish line, but

her team, with Rudy, Crazy Trevor and Bronte, finally came in fifth – only just taking them through into the final.

'I am so sorry, guys, I really let you down,' puffed Ugenia. 'I'm simply not good enough to be on the team. Maybe you should find someone else. You're never going to win a trophy with me on board.' Ugenia felt very disappointed with herself.

'Don't worry, you're just a bit out of practice. You need a little training, that's all,' said Rudy. 'We have a week or two, so we can start training tomorrow morning.'

'Oh, OK,' said Ugenia, who was half hoping that she would be allowed to quit as it all sounded like a lot of hard work. There must be easier ways to win a trophy, she thought.

Mrs Flitt had given some of the class other tasks to do during the Olympics. These tasks included raking the large sandpit after each long jump was measured, holding one end of the finishing line for the running races, and serving light refreshments.

As well as doing the relay race, Ugenia had been given the job of serving tarberry juice on the day of the finals. It was just a shame that there was no trophy for doing that, because Ugenia was sure she could win easily.

Ugenia felt a bit glum after school and, on her way home, decided to stop by Rudy's house for some encouragement. Rudy lived two streets away from Ugenia's house, on Leavesden Road, where the

houses were all squashed together like cheese-and-pickle sandwiches. Rudy lived right on the corner above his parents' shop, which was called Patels' Food Stores (only it didn't just sell food, it sold newspapers, Sellotape and weird things like pliers).

Ugenia decided she would buy a big bottle of tarberry juice and a Fizzy Martian ice pop. All that exercise had made her extremely thirsty and she needed to refuel her energy.

As she went to pay Rudy's dad for her shopping, Ugenia noticed a big sign on a noticeboard by the till. It said:

Ugenia stared at the words 'Win a trophy!' and thought about her great-grandad Freddy Lavender's trophy cabinet and how he'd won a trophy by growing a leek.

Maybe I could grow a leek or a marrow or something. After all, that's what my great-grandad did, thought Ugenia. And besides, I bet it's a much easier way to

win a trophy than by running in a relay race.

Then Ugenia stared at the words 'This SATURDAY'.

'Oh no, that's tomorrow! How on earth am I going to grow a vegetable in time? Oh well, maybe I . . .'

Ugenia stopped – a large green melon had caught her attention out of the corner of her eye.

Then suddenly, like a thunderbolt of lightning, Ugenia had a brainwave. 'Ingenious!' she cried. 'I'll buy one instead of growing one. No one will ever know the difference!'

So Ugenia decided to spend her pocket money on the large melon instead of the tarberry juice and ice pop. She picked up the heavy fruit and carried it over to the counter.

'Hello, Ugenia, that's one pound,' said Mr Patel.

'Oh, I only have eighty pence, Mr Patel! Can I owe it to you? It's really important!' cried Ugenia.

'Oh, very well,' said Mr Patel, sighing.

'Thanks, Mr Patel,' said Ugenia as she lifted the heavy melon and ran through the shop and up the stairs into the Patels' kitchen to show Rudy.

Rudy was tucking into a raisin naan bread.

'Rudy! Look at my melon!' Ugenia

cried. 'I'm going to win a trophy tomorrow morning, for my trophy cabinet. You have to come with me!' And Ugenia hopped round the kitchen with the enormous melon in her arms.

'Ugenia, we're meant to be training tomorrow. Have you forgotten we've got a race to win?'

Ugenia stopped jumping. 'Rudy, the race isn't for more than a week and, besides, I *have* to do this. You're going in for more than one event – you have the obstacle race as well as the relay – so I have to try to win the King of the Green Fingers competition. I mean, I've got to ensure I win a trophy for something too, right?' explained Ugenia.

'OK then, but we have to start training straight after that,' said Rudy, continuing

to munch his naan bread. 'And I've got a question, Ugenia. Where did you grow that melon? Or rather, where on earth did you get it?'

'What difference does it make where I got it, so long as I've got a fantastic fruit or vegetable to show?' asked Ugenia defensively.

'Well, the whole point of the competition is that you must have *grown* it,' said Rudy, grinning.

'So how are they going to know, anyway? Where I got the melon is just a small detail, right?' Ugenia muttered.

'OK, whatever you say!' giggled Rudy as he took an extra-large bite of his naan bread.

☆

Next morning, Ugenia and Rudy marched into the Community Centre, Ugenia proudly holding her large green melon.

They stood behind a long queue of people who were registering their names with their fruit or vegetables.

There were various neighbours of Ugenia's and Rudy's in the queue:

Mrs Murtle with some Cox's apples, Mr Horlix with his peas, Timothy Britain with his tomatoes, Shelley Clarkson with a cucumber, Kimberly Carrington with some carrots, Steven Sellers with a box of strawberries, Damian Goldsmith with some Granny Smith apples – and Ugenia Lavender with her large green melon.

'Rudy, I'm bound to win! Mine is totally the biggest fruit or veg!' whispered Ugenia, proudly hugging her melon and writing her name on the entry form.

After a while, all the entrants, including Ugenia, were directed up on to the stage and stood in a line as the judge, called Mr Nigel Greensleeves, began staring at their displays of fruit and vegetables with a very intense expression.

'Hmm, yes, very nice apple skin – a fine, shapely tomato . . .' said Mr Greensleeves, making his way along the row. Then he stopped at Ugenia's large green melon and stared at it. 'This is very interesting! Where on earth did you grow this huge melon?' he asked her.

'Er, in my garden, of course,' replied Ugenia, who had no idea where or how to grow a melon.

'Oh, really? That's extraordinary. I'm amazed you could have grown it without a greenhouse,' said Mr Greensleeves, frowning as he picked up Ugenia's melon and began to inspect it.

'Why on earth is there a price sticker on your melon saying "special price one pound"?' Mr Greensleeves asked suspiciously.

'Er, I don't know.' Ugenia tried her best and most innocent smile.

'Hmm, well, this is looking very odd to me,' said Mr Greensleeves crossly, and moved on to inspect Timothy Britain's tomatoes.

Ten minutes later, Mr Greensleeves had looked at all the entries. He stood very seriously with his clipboard and coughed to get everyone's attention. There was a hush at the Community Centre as the tension grew. Ugenia stared at the silver trophy, which stood gleaming on a little table next to the judge and the other organizers.

'And the winner of the King of the Green Fingers award is . . . Kimberly Carrington, with her magnificent carrots,'

Mr Greensleeves announced, handing the silver trophy to a very excited Kimberly.

'Injustice!' said Ugenia crossly.

'The rest of you won't go away empty-handed,' the judge declared. 'You will each receive a lovely big bag of fertilizer on your way out!'

'Fertilizer? What on earth do I want that for? I can't put that in my trophy cabinet!' huffed Ugenia.

Rudy took Ugenia's arm and guided her out of the door. They both dragged the big bag of fertilizer along behind them. Ugenia was about to explode with disappointment.

'Look, we have other things to think about right now – like training for the Boxmore Olympics,' said Rudy.

'Oh yeah, of course,' said Ugenia

glumly as they made their way to Boxmore Hill Green.

Rudy was keen not to let Ugenia dwell on her defeat – and even more keen to get her training for the relay. When they reached the green, they dumped the bag of fertilizer and Rudy made Ugenia start running up and down.

'Come on, Ugenia, just a little faster – you can do it!' yelled Rudy, trying to give Ugenia encouragement.

The following week, Ugenia began training with Rudy for half an hour every day after school – running round Boxmore Hill Green with Misfit. Misfit also needed training – he sometimes behaved like a little hooligan as he chased the other dogs.

Ugenia found all the training a huge effort and secretly couldn't really be bothered. She only went on with it because she desperately wanted to win a trophy so she could have a load of trophies like her great-grandad. She also didn't want to let Rudy down – he was so desperate to win the relay race.

The end of term – and the Boxmore Hill School Olympics – was fast approaching, and everyone had stepped up their training. The whole school was really excited – all except for Ugenia, who felt just like a really glum slug about the whole thing.

By the end of the school week, Ugenia was exhausted with all the training. She decided to pay Granny Betty a visit with Misfit. Ugenia always felt better after seeing her gran.

When Ugenia got to Granny Betty's, her gran's friend Mrs Wisteria was there. Mrs Wisteria was a skinny woman with white hair tightly pulled back in a bun. She was sitting on the couch with Rupert, her pristine white miniature poodle. She was brushing the dog's fur very vigorously.

Granny Betty went out into the kitchen to make some tea.

'Hi, Mrs Wisteria,' said Ugenia. 'Wow, you're certainly giving Rupert a good grooming.'

'Hello, dear,' Mrs Wisteria said, smiling at Ugenia. 'Rupert and I are just getting ready for the Boxmore Dog Show. 'We're in tip-top shape – all ready to win a very nice trophy.'

Ugenia's ears immediately pricked up. 'A trophy? You said a *trophy*?' Ugenia suddenly felt extremely excited. Here was another trophy that could be won in an easier way than by running.

'Yes, Rupert is top favourite to win! Actually, there's not much competition. Not many dogs are entered. You seem

quite interested – why not come along and watch? It's at ten o'clock tomorrow morning at the town hall.'

'I'm there! No, *we're* there!' said Ugenia, giving Misfit a hug.

'What do you mean? You can't bring that little rat!' laughed Mrs Wisteria snootily.

Misfit's extra-long tongue appeared and he started panting excitedly through his mop of messy hair.

'Yes I can! In fact, I'm going to enter him for the dog show. Misfit's got a very good personality!' snapped Ugenia proudly just as Granny Betty came in with a tray of tea and cakes.

'Granny Betty, Misfit and I are going to win the trophy at the dog show tomorrow. We're going home now as we have some

grooming to do.'

'Good for you! Good luck!' smiled Granny Betty.

Ugenia took Misfit back home to Cromer Road and gave him a long, soapy bath. Then she brushed through his tangled moppy hair, which he didn't like at all. Misfit hated being clean, so as soon as he was out of the bath he ran into the garden and rolled in a muddy puddle. Then he poked his extra-long tongue out and wagged his tail proudly.

On Saturday morning Ugenia did her early morning training with Rudy and then they went to the town hall with Misfit. Ugenia felt very excited as she eagerly queued up to enter the contest. She was very proud of Misfit and all ready to win a gleaming award for her trophy cabinet.

Ugenia stared at all the other people and their dogs. She gulped. There was Peanut the Pomeranian, Milly the Maltese, Gertrude the greyhound, Charlie the chihuahua, Desmond the dachshund, Ruby the red setter, Candy the cocker spaniel, Carlos the King Charles spaniel, Dallas the Dalmatian, Silver the springer spaniel, Bobby the Border collie, Petra the Pekinese – and Mrs Wisteria's poodle. They all looked perfectly immaculate – all except for Misfit, who was covered in encrusted mud from yesterday's roll, despite Ugenia's attempts to clean him off, and was drooling at the mouth with excitement.

The head judge, Mrs Penelope Winterbottom, began to inspect the dogs. 'Yes, a very nice coat . . . let's see his trick. Roll over!'

Ugenia watched as the other dogs performed obediently. She gulped again.

Finally, Mrs Winterbottom called Ugenia and Misfit out of the line.

Ugenia lifted Misfit on to the table for inspection.

'Now who on earth do we have here?' asked Mrs Winterbottom, and she began to prod Misfit as if he had a contagious illness.

'This is Misfit and I'm Ugenia Lavender,' said Ugenia. 'He really is a friendly, cosy and very lovable pet.' Misfit rolled over with delight, ready for his tummy tickle, and then gave Mrs Winterbottom a very big, sloppy kiss.

'Ugh, well, that's very nice for you, dear,' said Mrs Winterbottom as she wiped her mouth. 'I'm a little confused though – what breed is Misfit?'

'Er, I don't know exactly,' Ugenia said. 'I got him for my birthday from a dog pound. He might be a mix between a shih-tzu and a sheepdog – that's why he's so clever.'

'You mean he's a mutt! I'm afraid we don't have mutts in this competition,' Mrs Winterbottom announced haughtily, and she pulled a disgusted face as if she'd eaten something awful.

'Well, I think that's very unfair! There is nothing wrong in being a mix – it gives you a great personality!' said Ugenia defiantly.

But before Ugenia had a chance to state her case for Misfit winning the trophy, Mrs Winterbottom cleared her throat loudly.

'Ladies and gentlemen, thank you all for coming. You will all receive two free

cans of dog food for your efforts. But there can only be one winner of the Boxmore Dog Show trophy for the most remarkable, impeccable, lovable, adorable dog in the show.'

The hall hushed with excitement and tension.

'AND THE WINNER IS . . . Mrs Helena Doogie Jones with Dallas the Dalmatian!'

'Injustice!' cried Ugenia. 'That's so unfair! All I get left with are two cans of dog food, which I certainly cannot put in my trophy cabinet! I'm sorry, Misfit. It looks like she has really bad taste. Don't worry – I still think you're gorgeous.' And she gave Misfit a reassuring hug.

But before Ugenia had time to put Misfit

back on his lead, the puppy had jumped off the table and done a large stinky poo in Mrs Winterbottom's handbag when she wasn't looking.

Ugenia quickly grabbed Misfit and her two free cans of dog food. Rudy, Ugenia and Misfit walked swiftly out of the town hall before Mrs Winterbottom had a chance to notice the stinky thank-you present Misfit had left for her.

'Don't worry about it – we can use these cans of dog food for training,' said Rudy, and he began lifting them up as if they were dumb-bells.

Ugenia felt very tense all the rest of Saturday. There was only a day now before the Boxmore Olympics. The relay race on Monday afternoon was her last chance to win a trophy for her cabinet, and to make matters worse her whole family was coming to watch.

What if I lose? Not only will I have no trophy for my cabinet, but I will be losing in front of the whole school and my family! The only award I'll get will be the biggest loser award! she thought anxiously.

So Ugenia decided to spend Sunday preparing as best she could for Monday's big race. She ran around Boxmore Hill Green as fast as she could with Misfit and Rudy. She drank loads of orange juice, ate loads of pasta and cleaned her favourite

black trainers (at least she could look good for the occasion). She went to bed really early on Sunday night so she would be full of beans the next day, all ready and with plenty of energy for the relay-race final with Rudy, Bronte and Crazy Trevor.

On Monday afternoon the school field was packed with the family and friends of Boxmore Hill School's pupils, including Ugenia's parents, Uncle Harry and Granny Betty, who sat excitedly on benches, all ready to cheer on Ugenia and her friends. Misfit was there too, panting and barking enthusiastically.

The crowd was buzzing when Mrs Flitt finally came out and blew her whistle to start the first race, which was the hundred-

metre sprint. Rudy would probably have won it easily if he'd entered, but he'd decided to save himself for the relay and obstacle races.

Crazy Trevor came second in his long jump, and Bronte came third in her egg-and-spoon race, so they both received runners-up medals.

The crowd cheered and clapped after each event. Ugenia kept herself busy serving glasses of tarberry juice in a rather grumpy manner until it was time for the relay race. She was feeling increasingly nervous.

When Bronte took her position to run the first fifty metres of the relay, the atmosphere

was so electric the air was practically zinging and you could almost cut it. Trevor, Rudy and Ugenia waited in their positions ready to receive the baton.

Ugenia held her breath. This was her last chance to win a trophy for her cabinet.

Suddenly Mrs Flitt said, 'On your marks, get set, GOOOOO!'

Bronte ran as fast as she could, sprinting up to Crazy Trevor and handing him the baton. Then Crazy Trevor charged through his fifty metres, legging it as fast as he could and handing the baton to Rudy.

The crowd cheered – they were way ahead of everyone else. Ugenia gasped – they were bound to win now. Even she couldn't lose with a lead like this! Rudy surged towards her, but just as he thrust the baton into her hand, he lost his balance and tumbled on top of her. They both fell into a heap on the ground. Rudy shrieked and gripped his ankle in pain.

Ugenia lay flat on her back, watching in horror as the other teams sped past and her last chance of winning a trophy disappeared.

Rudy began to howl. 'I'm so sorry, Ugenia. I messed it up!' he said as he struggled to his feet and hobbled over to the nurse at the side of the track. Bronte and Crazy Trevor ran over and huddled round him. Ugenia walked slowly over to join them.

'Don't worry, Rudy,' said Ugenia sadly as she tried to cover up her disappointment. 'I'll go and get you some tarberry juice.'

Ugenia felt very glum as she wandered over to Granny Betty, who was waving from the bench.

'Oh, Granny Betty, I'm such a loser,'

Ugenia said sadly. 'I haven't won anything. I failed at the fruit and vegetable competition and the dog show, and now poor Rudy has hurt himself. All our training was for nothing, and we've lost the relay race. I feel like a total loser. I tried so hard to win loads of trophies like Great-grandad Freddy Lavender, but I can't turn my hand to anything. I'm just useless!'

'Ugenia, your great-grandad used to say, "The only losers are the ones so afraid of failure they don't even try,"' Granny Betty said gently, giving Ugenia a hug. 'Now, stop feeling sorry for yourself and go and give some support to your friend Rudy.'

Ugenia picked up a carton of tarberry juice and ran back to Rudy, who was getting his ankle bandaged by the school

nurse. Ugenia handed Rudy the juice.

'Thanks, Ugenia,' he said. 'I'm sorry we didn't get to win you a trophy. It's all my fault.'

'Don't worry, Rudy, it's the taking part that counts. And we tried, didn't we? Right?' said Ugenia.

'Yeah, but I can't even run my obstacle race now. My ankle's really sore. It's a shame because I was really looking forward to it and it's the last race in the competition. There's still a trophy to be won.'

Ugenia stared at Rudy. Suddenly, like a thunderbolt of lightning, she had a brainwave. 'Incredible!' she cried. 'Maybe I could do your obstacle race for you. I might as well try – we haven't got anything to lose, have we?'

'You're right, Ugenia. Go for it!' laughed Rudy. 'This one's yours!' And Bronte and Crazy Trevor grinned and nodded. They all knew how desperately Ugenia wanted to win a trophy.

Mrs Flitt decided to let Rudy choose his own replacement, so Ugenia tied her trainers extra tight and jogged determinedly towards the starting line. The other contestants were already limbering up for what was going to be the hardest and most challenging race of the whole Boxmore Olympics.

Mrs Flitt blew her whistle and shouted, 'On your marks, get set, GOOOOO!'

Ugenia ran faster than she ever had before, trying desperately to keep up with the others. This race was extra long,

involving various challenges along the way.

Ugenia was behind all the other runners as they ran around the track. When they'd wriggled through the tunnels there were three people ahead of her – Sebastian, Max and Liberty. Chantelle was behind her.

Ugenia tried to keep a steady pace as there was still a long way to go. As they dribbled the football around the cones there were two people in front of her – Sebastian and Max. Liberty and Chantelle were behind her.

Ugenia kept taking deep breaths, still trying to keep her pace steady as they entered the section where they each had to grab a beanbag and run with it on their heads.

As they reached the final leg of the race,

Max, Liberty and Chantelle were behind Ugenia and only Sebastian was still ahead.

Suddenly Ugenia could see the finish line, but she was still in second place. She began to feel tired and frustrated – but then she thought of Freddy Lavender's words: 'The only losers are the ones so afraid of failure they don't even try.'

As she let her great-grandad's words fill her mind, Ugenia felt herself turning into a supersonic rocket. She started running like she'd never run before, steaming straight past Sebastian and on through the finish line.

The crowd roared, and Granny Betty and all the Lavender family clapped and cheered. Bronte, Crazy Trevor and Rudy, who had hobbled over to a bench to

FINISH

watch with the others, were screaming and shouting.

When the exhausted runners had jogged over to her, Mrs Flitt blew her whistle and got everyone's attention.

'I would like to thank everyone taking part today. You'll all be going home with a medal, but I have one more trophy to hand out – to the winner of the hardest and longest race of the Boxmore Hill School Olympics. It took real stamina and commitment to win that race. AND THE WINNER IS . . . UGENIA LAVENDER!'

Ugenia leaped into the air with excitement as she ran over to Mrs Flitt, took a huge bow, punched the air in victory and grabbed the shiny silver trophy.

'This trophy really belongs to someone

else,' Ugenia said, and she handed it to Rudy. 'If it wasn't for Rudy I wouldn't have run this race in the first place. He encouraged me to take part in the Boxmore Olympics and he helped me to train every day so I was fit enough. So thanks, Rudy!' And Ugenia smiled and gave Rudy a big hug as everyone cheered and clapped.

'Thanks, Ugenia, that was really kind of

you,' said Rudy quietly. 'Because I know you wanted a trophy for your own trophy cabinet.'

'Rudy, I don't even *own* a trophy cabinet,' giggled Ugenia, and with that she ran off to do her victory lap of honour.

Big News!

Hi there, everyone!

I can hardly write this news update. I'm soooooo excited! So many amazing things are happening in my life. Can you believe it? I won!!!!!!! I won, I won! It's a miracle!

Maybe I do take after my great-grandfather Freddy Lavender after all. I'm working now on getting my own trophy cabinet – well, maybe a trophy shelf!

I know it sounds a bit cheesy, but I feel like a winner for more than just running the race. I have so many fantastic friends in my life – like Rudy, who really supported me through training, which made it just so cool to give him my trophy. And then there's Bronte and Crazy Trevor. And my Granny Betty. Do you love her or what?! Isn't she just so cool for an old person? I mean, she doesn't behave like an old person normally does. Yeah, she is very wise, but she still remembers to have fun, which I think is really important.

Anyway, I've decided that since I'm in such a good mood I'm actually going to help my mum with the housework. As if! Well, I might tidy up my room just to be nice.

Oh, I forgot to tell you about Misfit. He is living up to his name, big time. As well as doing a poo in that snooty lady's handbag at the dog show, he has decided that he needs to be carried down the stairs all the time. He barks furiously until someone lifts him up. If he had a voice he'd scream, 'Carry me! I can't be bothered!'

Don't tell anyone, but yesterday I smuggled Misfit into the twenty-four-hour, bargain-budget, bulk-buyers' supersized supermarket in my luminous rucksack. Nobody noticed!

Anyway, see you soon – gotta go!

Big X0

Ugenia Lavender XX

Ingenious Top Tip

In order to win, you have to play the game

I know it sounds obvious, but if I don't try at something I'm definitely not going to win it. Or, in fact, achieve anything. Sometimes, trying new things is scary – but you're only a real loser if you don't even try.

Brain Squeezers

Magpie's Missing Words

I lost count of all the magpies I saw on Friday the thirteenth, but it didn't matter, as it turned out to be a really lucky day for me after all! Can you remember the rhyme Granny Betty told me about magpies? Fill in the missing words to complete the lines.

'One for sorrow,

_ _ _ for joy,

Three for a girl,

Four for a _ _ _,

_ _ _ _ for silver,

Six for _ _ _ _,

Seven for a _ _ _ _ _ that's never been told.'

Tip! If you're stuck, turn to page 65.

Ugenia's Shopping Search

Do you remember the day Bronte's mum took us shopping to Garrods, the most glamorous shop in the world? I've never seen so many different things to buy in one place! Can you find seven of them in my shopping wordsearch? The words can be up, down, backwards, forwards or even diagonal!

HANDBAG PANTS POODLE
POTATOES RING SHOES SOFA

S P O T A T O E S
U A H P E I G L E
G N I R M A T U O
O T U H B F N E B
I S K D P M L I S
B E N G J D U Q H
G A L D O S T A O
H O S O D U B I E
S H P L T A F O S

Ugenia's Green-fingered Grid

OK, I admit that I cheated in the King of the Green Fingers Gardening competition, but I'll never do it again – promise! To find out which fruit I took to the competition, look at the clues below. All of them are names of fruit or vegetables. Can you write the five words across the grid? If you do, my fruit will be revealed in the vertical box.

1. Round and red, this is great in salads and sandwiches. But is it a fruit or a vegetable?

2. Small, red and juicy, this fruit tastes great with cream and sugar. Mmm!

3. This fruit can be red or green, but it's always crunchy and delicious. When you eat it, just leave the core.

4. You can eat this vegetable raw or cooked. It's orange and is a rabbit's favourite food!

5. This round fruit must be peeled before you eat it. Its name is exactly the same as its colour!

Ugenia's Lucky Letters

Granny Betty's beautiful silver charm bracelet has got many lucky charms hanging from it. Can you remember five of them? The words are below – but all the 'e's and 'a's are missing. Can you put them back in to spell the words correctly?

Magpie's Missing Words

Two
boy
Five
gold
story

Ugenia's Green-fingered Grid

				1 t	o	**m**	a	t	o
2 s	t	r	a	w	b	**e**	r	r	y
			3 a	p	p	**l**	e		
		4 c	a	r	r	**o**	t		
			5 o	r	a	**n**	g	e	

Ugenia's Shopping Search

S P O T A T O E S
U A H P E I G L E
G N I R M A T U O
O T U H B F N E B
I S K D P M L I S
B E N G J D U Q H
G A L D O S T A O
H O S O D U B I E
S H P L T A F O S

Ugenia's Lucky Letters

elephant
cat
feather
car
daisy

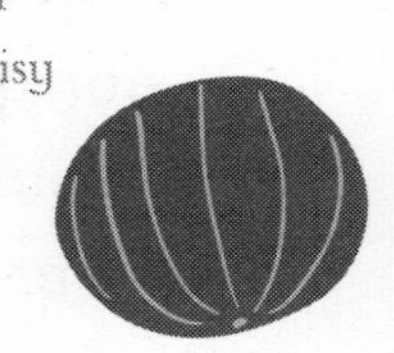

Answers

Ugenia Lavender is moving to 13 Cromer Road. How will she fit in as the new girl at school? Does she ever discover the meaning of the Lovely Illness? And can she rescue celebrity chef Uncle Harry from a big mix-up?

When Ugenia Lavender meets Elsa at the travelling circus, can she prove that the terrible tiger is more of a purring pussycat? And how will she stop arch-enemy Lara Slater from being a Leading Lady Thief? Does Ugenia stay the most popular girl in the school? Or will it be more a case of Ugenia Lavender, Who Do U Think U R?

Ugenia Lavender is off on holiday. What's it like being stranded on a desert island? Will she get back from holiday in time to ride the scariest ride ever at the Lunar Park Funfair? And just how will she get back to school in one piece? That depends on what happens when Ugenia is left Home Alone . . .

Ugenia is convinced there is a real live giant living next door to her Granny Betty. But just how does she prove it? And can she stop her parents from being taken in by a beautiful bloodsucker? Just as Ugenia thinks it can't get any worse she finds herself stuck in the Temple of Gloom. Will she ever find a way out?

Ugenia Lavender has discovered that the planet is fast running out of energy. But luckily she has a plan to save the day. How can she help an alien return to outer space? And what happens when she meets her hero, Hunk Roberts? Does it make up for the fact that Ugenia might no longer be the One and Only?

Incredible praise for Ugenia Lavender!

'You know Geri the Spice Girl, now meet Geri the author!' *Sun*

'[A] lovable heroine' *Sunday Express*

'It's inspirational! It's totally ingenious!' *Independent on Sunday*

'[Geri] has created a heroine who is strong, sassy, believable . . .' *Mail on Sunday*

'Be enchanted by Geri Halliwell's children's book, *Ugenia Lavender*' *Daily Express*